Esme's Life as a Ten-Year-Old!

I0157048

Written and Illustrated
By
Vicki Baxter

First Published in 2024 by Blossom Spring Publishing
Esme's Life as a Ten-Year-Old!© 2024 Vicki Baxter
ISBN 978-1-0687019-3-1
E: admin@blossomspringpublishing.com
W: www.blossomspringpublishing.com

For Esme and Hattie.
My inspiring girls.
Sparkle forever.

Hi everyone,

I've written a story for you all. I hope you like it. I thought you might want to read a bit about what I get up to each day. I've put some really funny stuff in here, I bet it makes you laugh. I hope the sad bits don't make you cry, or the annoying bits make you angry though.

  I wonder what part you will like best, or if you feel the same way about things as I do.
  Anyway, happy reading!

Love Esme.

About me, Esme.

I'm Esme and I turned ten years old on the twenty-sixth of March. I finally have my ears pierced and I have collected so many earrings already, most of them were birthday presents though. I had to wait until my birthday to get them done as my Mum wouldn't let me do it any sooner. I want second piercings now!

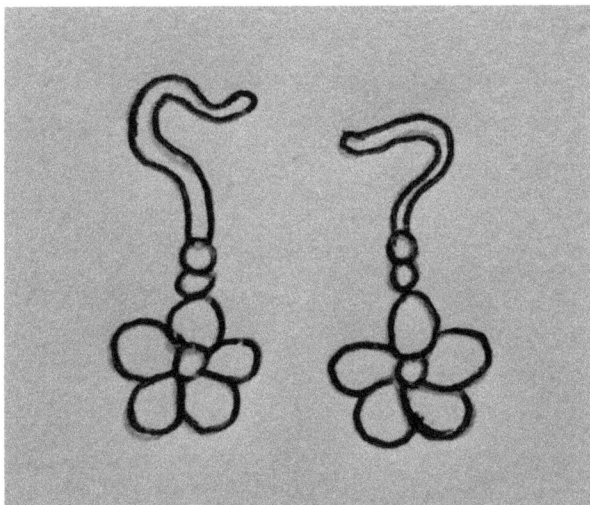

I have a younger sister called Hattie; she turns seven next month. Hattie is already asking Mum to get her ears pierced. I keep telling her there is no hope, seeing as I had to wait a billion years for mine. I had them done with a needle at a piercing and tattoo studio, it hurt so much, but they healed really quickly.

I don't understand why Mum won't let me get a second piercing, all my friends are getting their second and some their third ones done, and I have to wait until I am fifteen! Someone asked me the other day if I wanted the next piercing done for me, or because all my friends have them. I didn't know the answer to that.

Me and Hattie share a room, but not for too much longer. We are getting an extension built at Mum's house and we will get our own bedrooms then. I can't wait, her trafs (traf is fart spelt backwards) stink, Hattie's not Mum's! I've already chosen my cactus bedding and wall art for my new room.

We will still share a room at Dad's house, but that's ok because we aren't in bunk beds there. We have bunk beds at Mum's and I'm on the bottom, so every time

Hattie moves it sounds like she is going to crash down on top of me and when she trafs, it's like it comes down into my face.

One day Dad is going to change his lounge, and dining room bit into a bedroom for me by putting up a wall and giving me a door too. I hope my cat doesn't rub her bum on my face if she sleeps in with me. She never really goes upstairs, so she might like the company of me being down in the lounge area with her.

We have a rabbit called Muffin at Mum's house. We thought she was a boy, but the vet told us she was a girl when Mum took her there to have 'him fixed.' This was meant to calm him down a bit because he/she is really naughty. We have two guinea pigs too. Mine is Pancake and Hattie's is Syrup. We got them in lockdown, so I'm not sure if they will live that much longer.

We only have one cat at Dad's now. Gertie is mine. When Mum and Dad split up, we had to give Cybil away, she was Hattie's. Dad said he couldn't take both the cats because they didn't get on very well. Cybil was younger and we think it made Gertie jealous when she arrived as a kitten and got loads of attention. Mum said she couldn't have one either because there was no place to put a cat flap in the new house. So, Cybil had to go. I still feel sad about this sometimes, even though she was Hattie's.

I get sad about my Grandad sometimes too. He is in heaven now. I didn't see him much because he lived about six hours' drive away and Dad found it quite hard to take us up there when we were younger. He was still my Grandad though and I miss him. It makes me cry when I think about him at bedtime. Mum bought a mole statue with a moustache that looks like him, we keep it at Dads on his front doorstep. It is called Grandad mole.

Life is ok now we have two houses. Mum and Dad used to argue a lot in the old house. I hated it and was always telling them to stop arguing, even though they were in another room hiding their words from me, I could still hear the noise of it. Hattie doesn't remember that because she was too young. Sometimes she still finds it hard and wants us all to live together in one house.

Mum always says, 'no way' and tries to explain how it is better to have two happy parents in two houses than living with two miserable ones in one house. *It was a bungalow actually, Mum*! I miss the old bungalow (The Bunghole my parents called it). I had a big bedroom all to myself, a huge trampoline in the garden and a garage for all of our stuff.

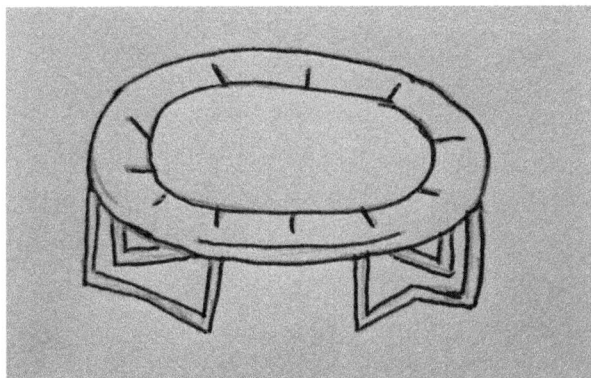

We go to a village primary school. I can never be bothered to get up in the morning and go, but mostly I have a good day at school with my friends... unless we have fallen out. Mum says over ridiculous things, but they are important to us.

My teacher last year thought we had lots of arguments because we didn't get the chance when we were in year three because of lockdown and homeschooling when it was Covid. Mum said he told her that, the usual falling out that happens in friendship groups mixed with our surging hormones, make the problems seem a lot bigger than they are.

You can even see the sea from the school field and probably the classroom windows too if I stand up on my chair. I wouldn't do that, I'm really good at school and never break the rules. I've got one year left and then I'll be moving to secondary school. I like to call it high school, like on TV.

I'm going to tell you a bit about what I get up to now. I hope you enjoy reading it. I wonder if you do the same things as me, or feel like I do sometimes. If this was on my YouTube channel, I'd ask you to like, subscribe and comment down below with your thoughts!

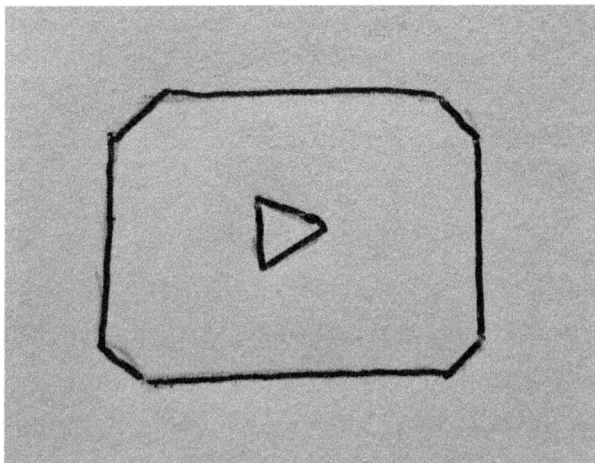

Chapter 1

School Morning

07:30-08:30. Mum comes in about 07:30am to wake me and Hattie up for school. Usually, I am really annoyed, it always feels so early, and I just want to stay in bed. Most of the time I pull the duvet over my head, but that doesn't stop her annoying me even more by opening the curtains or putting the lights on.

It feels like I have been lying there for about thirty seconds and she starts calling us with the five-second countdown. If we don't get our cereal in the next five seconds, then we would be ruining her perfectly good mood. Five, four, three...

We both always get there in time and open the cupboard to see what boring cereals there are to choose from. Raisin Wheats, Weetabix, Rice Crispies. Mum doesn't let us have Chocolate Pillows or nice cereals. Nanny does though and Dad gives us pancakes.

The best thing about breakfast is the vitamin pill. It's like having a Haribo sweet first thing when we wake up. Mum would never actually let us do that. We aren't even allowed screen time until we are completely dressed and ready for school. No, iPad or TV!

There's never enough time to get them either. Mum says it's because I spend too much time looking in the mirror or faffing with my hair. I don't! We are always rushed out of the house at about 08:30am for the school run.

Normally me or Hattie are still in the bathroom when Mum wants to lock the front door. This really gets on her wick she says. It always ends up with her yelling from the porch with her list of orders... 'teeth, hair, shoes, bag, car...let's go!'

08:30-08:50. The school run can go one of two ways. It depends how much we have messed about when Mum is trying to get us to leave the house. If we have, then when we are in the car, it usually starts with a lecture. Mum says she never wakes up in a bad mood, but we put her in it by not listening and doing what we are told.

I should probably add in here that Mum doesn't normally do the school run. Usually, we are dropped at Nanny and Grandpa's house for breakfast so Mum can head off to work. If she starts early, she can finish early, which means we only have to spend an hour in the after-school club before she picks us up. Mum isn't at work at the moment though because she is recovering from shoulder surgery. I wish she didn't have to go back, it's really nice having her around all the time.

Anyway, we just sit there in the car, quietly. She thinks we are feeling bad for upsetting her, but actually, we are just really bored of hearing it again, so just look out the window instead, or we talk to each other silently in the back seats without her realising.

If we left the house when Mum wanted us to, because we were super speedy at getting ready, then we have a blast on the school run. Mum sometimes burps us the alphabet, or we will sing stupid songs and have to guess what they are.

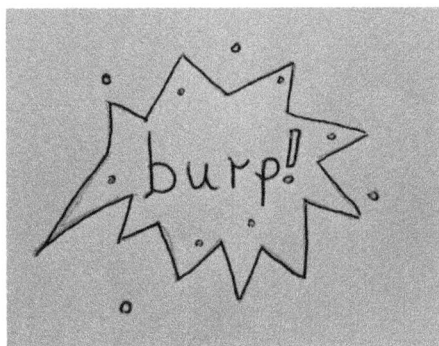

We get to school between 08:40 and 08:50 depending on traffic. We have never ever been late. Mum is always early for everything. Sometimes we have to sit there for a few minutes because the teachers haven't even opened the gates!

Mum always walks us across the road and gives us a kiss at the gate before we go in. She says, 'love you,' but normally her last words are 'put your hair up.' My friends wear their hair down all the time. Mum says it is the school rules because they don't want to spread nits. Mum always follows the school and uniform rules, which is annoying because my friends wear boots too and she won't let me, and we've never even had nits!

08:50-13:15. The school morning is pretty much the same every day. We leave Mum at the gates and when we get to the reception, Hattie walks right to her classroom and I go left to get to mine. The first thing I do is get my Squishmallows collectors book out of my bag and look at it at my desk. I sneak it in from home because Mum doesn't let me bring books, pens or notepads into school. All my friends do though.

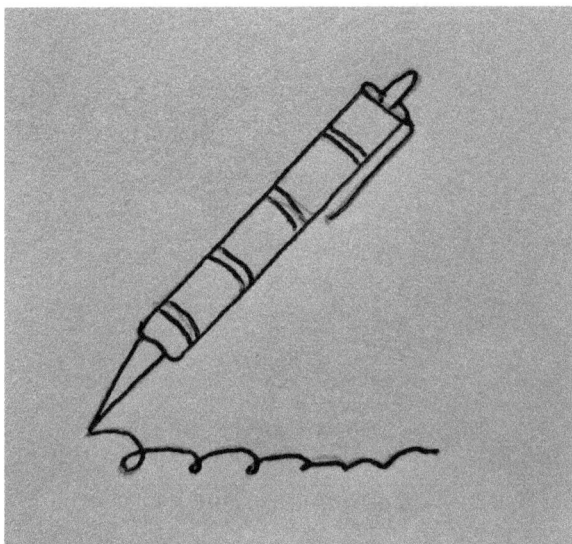

I watch my friends arrive. One time this really funny thing happened. We were meant to have a school movie day as a reward for being really good and we could bring in a pillow, blanket, and cuddly toy. Well, this boy in my class turned up with all his stuff in his arms and we were like 'What are you doing?' He said, 'Oh, it's movie day, this is my stuff,' and we all laughed because it wasn't actually until the next week!

At 09:00 the teacher calls the register. Sometimes some of the boys say stupid things when their names are called out, like spaghetti head or something, this really makes us laugh. I don't ever say anything weird though.

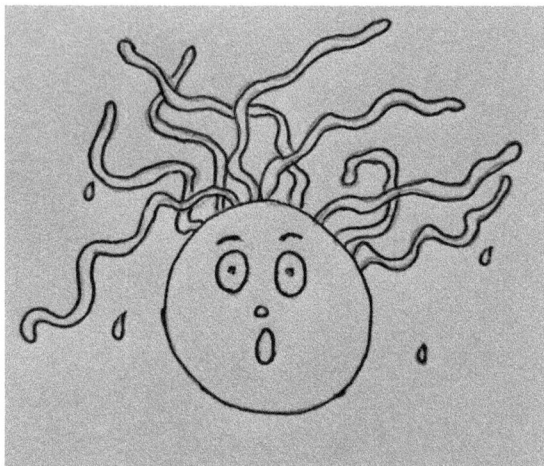

I try to be really helpful at school, I love getting merits and have got over one hundred and fifty already. When you reach one hundred, you get a different coloured star for each year you are in. I'm trying for two hundred to see what I get then. I have saved all of the class stars so far; I keep them at home in my memory box.

We do Maths first, then class reading, then have a fifteen minute break for a snack. Mum gives us crackers or yoghurt tubes, all my friends have chocolate and crisps, it is so annoying. We go outside to play and then we do literacy before lunchtime. I often ask the teacher if she wants my help handing out the LO's (learning objective slips) and books. This usually gets me a merit.

We watch the lessons on a PowerPoint and then we do the paperwork that goes with it. We aren't allowed to speak when the teaching video is on. Sometimes something funny will happen though, like the turtle that answers the questions on the screen and always gets them wrong and we all go, 'wonder what it will say wrong this time?' and then it was actually right!

When we do our reading aloud in class everyone gets to have a go. We read from one punctuation and stop at the next so the next person can start. Sometimes the boys will read it in a really silly voice or do stupid actions, which makes us all laugh a bit.

We have our break and lunchtime in the playground and school field. I play with my friends, and we do singing challenges or play escape Granny games. Sometimes we play twenty-one dares. This can be really embarrassing. Some of the things that have been done (not by me though) are, going up to a boy and asking him if he can teach you how to play football, or going up to a year six and saying 'I like you' to him.

When it is our turn for the dinner hall we get called in by the teacher and when we have finished eating, we can go back out and play again. Mum makes me have cooked school dinners. I really want a packed lunch like my friends, but Mum says she hasn't got time in her life to be making them every single day.

Mum orders the school meal choices online before the school term. She likes us to try new things and if we come home and say it was totally disgusting, then she will change it to another option for the next week. The puddings are always nice, but the pasta can be dry, and some things are just too spicy.

Sometimes the kitchen gets it wrong and gives me something I know Mum hasn't ordered for me, or they have run out by the time I get there, so I have to have something else that's gross. Mum gets really annoyed when this happens and e-mails the school. She says what is the point of her prepaying and being organised enough to put the option in for an entire half term if you don't even get what you have ordered anyway.

When me and my friends are in silly moods, we sit in the dinner hall and yell out. My friend shouted out 'Domino-o-oh' and I sometimes sing 'Yodel-ay-yodel-ay-ee-oo'. We don't get into trouble, it's just funny.

Chapter 2

School afternoon

1:15-3:10 or 4:15. Depending on the day of the week, every school afternoon is different. We learn lots of different subjects each day. P.E (Physical Education), is on a Monday and Wednesday, other lessons we have are History, Geography, Art, Science, French, ICT (Information Communication Technology), PSHE (Personal, social, health and economics) and R.E (Religious Education).

Sometimes we have visitors come into the school to take us for the subject. We had a coach from the local cricket club come in once and take us for P.E. We have also had a nurse come in and teach us all about our bodies and changes and making babies. Mum had to sign a form to say she was happy for me to be in that class. I wish she hadn't said yes, it was so embarrassing.

The teacher wrote a note to all the parents after the sex education talk. Apparently, the nurse was really pleased with our knowledge and sensible attitude in the session and praised us for our good questions. I asked one, I wanted to know how you get twins. One of the boys asked a really embarrassing question. I think he already knew the answer and was just making the nurse explain 'everything' to us.

The nurse asked us to volunteer to draw a boy's private parts on the board and one of the boys did it so big, it was really funny. We were taught how to check our breasts for lumps, which can be caused by cancer. The lady had knitted boobs for that bit and was squeezing them, we were all laughing, she had lots of knitted body parts.

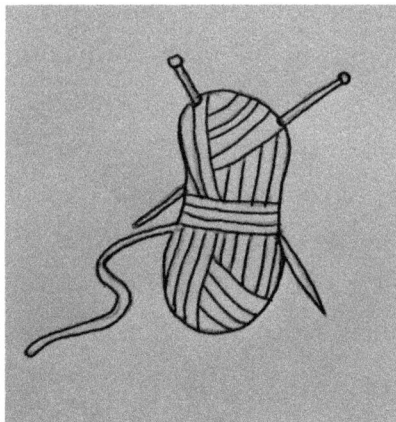

Art is probably my favourite lesson. Mum says I am really good at drawing, especially copying things. I did a Bob Ross painting lesson on YouTube once and Mum was so impressed she still has it stuck to the fridge at home. My Nan's uncle was an artist and so was Dad's Grandad, so I think it is in my blood. Hattie is really good too.

I used to hate P.E., especially running. I don't know why I did it, but sometimes the teacher comes into our lesson and asks for people to put their hands up if they want to take part in inter-school sports things. I put my hand up all the time and never got picked for anything decent like netball or surfing. What I did get picked for was cross country.

I didn't realise it at the time, but if you said you would do it, it wasn't just the one race, it was four and you had to be able to do all of them. I hated the first one so much. I cried afterwards as I had such a bad stitch and came something like seventy-eighth out of eighty people. I begged Mum not to give permission for me to go to the next one, but she said it is good to push through and to show commitment to something and your team, even if you really don't want to. Mum said even if I came last, finishing was the only important thing and trying my best.

I did run all four of them in the end and each time I got a slightly better score. The last one I ran I even came in the fifties and didn't hate it. Mum came and watched every single one and was super proud of me. Last sports day I didn't even finish the six laps of the school field, I gave up after two. This time I'm going to finish it because I know I can. I even ran a one-mile fun run with my friends in the holidays, but mostly I did that for the medal and a goody bag.

Some afternoons we go out on the school minibus to a pool and do swimming with the teachers. That is always good fun. We aren't supposed to eat on the coach, but I always sneak a snack and eat it sat really low down in my chair, so I don't get caught. We always fight to see who can get on first and get the back seats. They are the best.

On Fridays, we have a celebration assembly. Sometimes Mum sends us in with things for us to talk about on stage, like when I got my gold award at Brownies for getting all my badges. Hattie had her sash from Rainbows too and they called us up together in front of the school and all the parents and asked us about what we got them for. Hattie was so shy she barely spoke, so I had to do the talking for both of us. I could feel my face go red; I wish it didn't do that.

They always give the 'Star of the Week' out in assembly too. Two children in each year get it, but we never know who the teacher has picked until they call out the names. Mum says she will only come to assembly if she has a message to say one of us has won it, or if we are showing something.

When we walk in, me and Hattie always check to see if Mum is there, that way we always know if one of us has won 'Star of the Week.' Mum always gives us a thumbs up and is smiling like mad when we are on the stage getting it. We both have three each so far this year. Mine are for *making a super effort to read regularly at home, having a fantastic positive attitude in class* and *writing fantastic sentences using the spelling words in my homework.* Hopefully, I can get one more before we finish this year so I can beat Hattie.

Sometimes a class, or just a few of us, will perform something in the assembly. Everyone is supposed to be really quiet and sit nicely. Parents are even told that if they have small children with them that disrupt it, they need to leave quietly and take them outside the hall.

One time my friend was up on stage reading a poem she wrote in class and her two-year-old brother was shouting all the way through it and calling out her name. Then to make it worse, he ran away from his Dad and got up on the stage at the front and just stood there. We were all laughing so much. Mum said it was lucky the head teacher wasn't in that day, or she would've thrown them out!

School finishes at 3:10pm, but Mum doesn't get us from pick up except for on Wednesdays and Fridays. Mum doesn't work on a Friday and finishes early on a Wednesday so she can take us to Karate, we haven't been going long because we used to do Girl Guiding club instead, but when I finished Brownies, I wanted to do something different. We are doing our first grading next weekend to be a red belt.

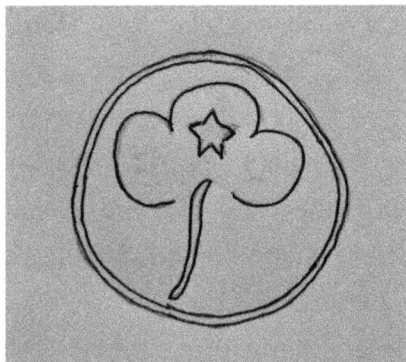

When Mum gets to the school, she waits outside Hattie's gate for us to meet her. We normally throw our coats at her and dump our bags at her feet for her to carry to the car. She always does it, asking, 'What am I... a donkey?' We always get a cuddle and kiss when we see her, so I don't think she minds really.

On a Monday I go to the after-school kids club, Hattie does hockey. It's quite fun as my friends go there too and we draw, play games or if it is nice weather play outside on the gym equipment, field or tennis court.

On Tuesday, I do drama and Hattie goes to Kids Club. We are rehearsing for a play at the moment that we will do with other schools in the massive theatre in the city. It's my first time doing that, and I have a speaking part, so I'm a bit nervous. Mum says to just look at the lights and balcony and not at people in the audience.

On Thursday I play cricket and Hattie does Book Club. I'm not really into it. I haven't done it before this term. Mum says I need to go because otherwise, she will have to pay for the Kids Club fees when she is working, so it saves her money and that means more money to spend on things we want like Squishmallows.

I was so upset on my first cricket session because I accidentally left my earrings in and when I was taking them out on the field, I dropped one. We all looked for it, but it was lost forever because they had only just mowed it and there was grass everywhere. Mum said I do get upset over silly things! She says that when I get annoyed because I can't put my hair up without it being lumpy, or when my socks don't feel comfortable. She doesn't understand.

Chapter 3

Weeknights at Mum's

Mum has us with her on a Monday and Wednesday evening. We sleep at Mum's every weeknight during term time because Dad gets up too early for work in the mornings. We don't really do much with Mum on her evenings, to be honest.

We get picked up at 4:15pm from school clubs on a Monday and 3:10pm from the gates on a Wednesday. Mum is always pleased to see us and gives us a kiss and cuddle and asks how our days have been. We normally just tell her it was good and get in the car to drive home.

Most of the time Mum has a snack waiting for us, this could be dried mango, lentil curls or sometimes even a small bag of sweets. If Mum has been rushing and forgets the snack, then we stop at the shop in the next village along from school and she runs in and gets us a surprise... normally a bag of Skips.

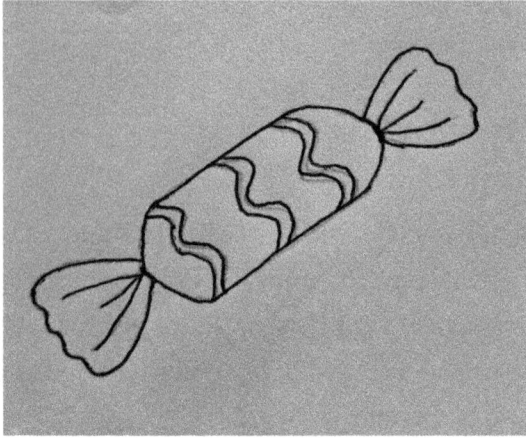

Hattie and I talk non-stop on the car journey home, not to each other, but to Mum. We talk at the same time too and Mum has to tell us to stop and only one of us speaks because she can't concentrate on what we are both saying and driving at the same time. She says all she can hear is, 'Mum! Mum! Mum!'

When we get home, we take off our shoes and dump our bags on the porch. Mum takes out any letters and reading books that we need to use that evening. Whilst she makes dinner, we usually grab our iPads (they are Samsung tablets actually, but we always say iPads) and headphones and chill on the sofa for a bit.

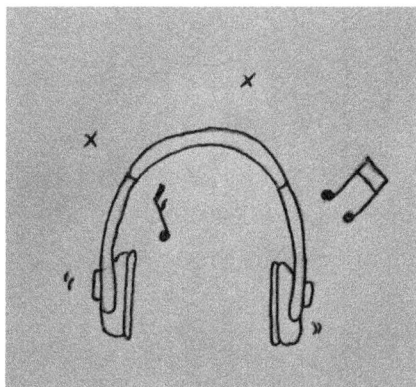

We all sit at the dinner table together and there is a no-screen rule whilst we eat. This is our time to chat. If Mum has made something and she isn't sure if we will like it (because she has made it up from the ingredients she found in the cupboards and fridge), she will put out our plates and stick it in a massive bowl in the middle so we can help ourselves to the amount we want.

Normally we will have fish fingers, potatoes and peas, chicken stir fry, tuna pasta, or picnic tea as Mum calls it, which is basically crackers, cream cheese, ham, salad vegetables and sliced up fruit with some bread. We eat these dinners quickly.

Sometimes Mum decides to make something new like her beetroot risotto. That was so bad we made her promise never, ever, to make it again, it took us ages to eat it. It can take Hattie up to a whole hour before she has finished her tiny portion sometimes. When we hate the dinner, we ask Mum to show us how much we have to eat before we can have pudding. Literally every mouthful is so disgusting that we get through so many cups of squash trying to swallow it down without tasting it.

Pudding can be anything from yoghurt, ice lollies, sliced up fruit, frozen banana or even flapjacks if we have made them and there are some left over. We make healthy flapjacks. I can do them myself now. We made up the recipe and it is really good. The ingredients we use are oats, honey, raisins, sliced apple, one egg, cinnamon, a splash of milk and a sprinkling of flour.

We don't do much on a Monday after dinner. If it is nice weather we might play out in the garden with the animals, or walk to the park, but mostly we chill out and have a game of Uno and watch a movie together. Resting after the weekend, Mum says.

Wednesdays are different because we go to Karate after an early dinner. Mum doesn't let us get changed into our outfits until we are about to leave the house because she says if we get them dirty, she would never be able to get them that white again! We are at the Dojo for one hour and fifteen minutes, parents aren't allowed to watch the training, just the gradings.

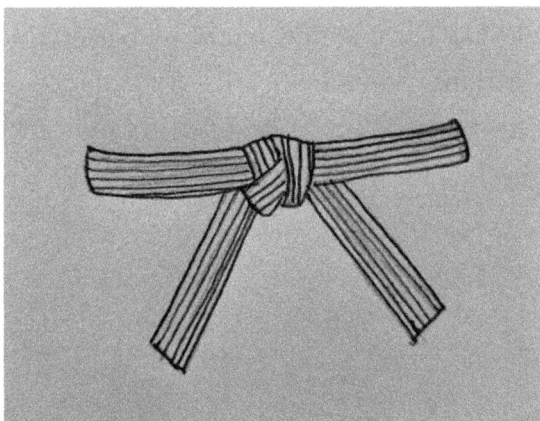

We are always hungry when we come out, but Mum won't let us snack until we are home, and our uniforms are safely back in the cupboard again. We normally have some cereal and then do some drawing or record YouTube videos in our room. Mum won't let me upload them until she has checked them for online safety though.

We have hair washes on a Sunday night with Mum, so we don't have them on her weeknight evenings, as we do alternate days. These fall when we are with Dad. I still have a shower before bed though. Mum sends us to bed at about 8:00 pm. We do our reading then, Hattie reads out loud every night and then Mum reads us a story too.

It's lights out at 8:30pm after we have done our final wee and she has given us a kiss and cuddle, but when I have my own room, I'm going to stay up until 9 pm reading. I just can't at the moment, because Hattie is younger than me. Sometimes, I ask if I can read under the covers with a torch, but Mum says it would disturb my sister and is bad for my eyesight.

Mum goes to bed when we do, but she doesn't go to sleep, she will read, or catch up on e-mails and watch grown-up Netflix on her iPad with her headphones. Me and Hattie always giggle and chat for about fifteen minutes after lights out. It gets Mum so cross, and she says things like, '*This is my time now, I need quiet so I can concentrate, go to sleep or you will be exhausted in the morning,*' and '*I'm warning you!*' This just makes us giggle even more.

Mum says she always checks on us at 10pm before she goes to sleep, and we are never awake. Sometimes she will adjust our covers and she will pull our door to, so it is only open a tiny bit. I get up for a wee in the night sometimes and Mum has told me the next day that we have had an entire conversation in the bathroom about nonsense because I have been half asleep. I don't remember it at all, it is so funny.

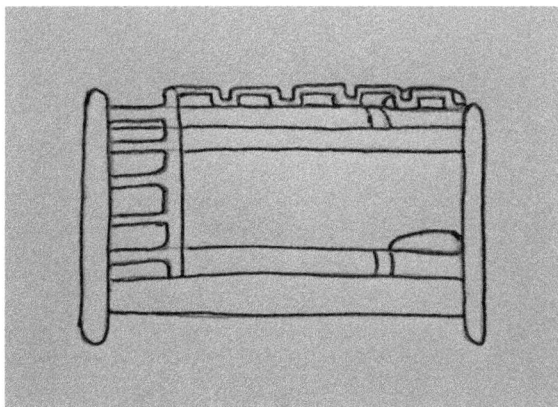

Mum said that some nights she has to come in, because one of us is dreaming, and we are talking in our sleep. When she tells us what we have been saying it is always really funny because it doesn't make any sense. One night Hattie was calling out and Mum said she found her next to the wall, sat on the floor trying to climb through the full-length mirror. Hattie loves hearing that story over and over again.

Chapter 4

Weeknights Dad

Dad works on a building site, so we don't stay overnight with him unless he has a holiday, because he would have to get us up too early on a school morning. He finishes at about 5 o'clock and depending on if he has cycled or driven, he will usually get us no later than quarter past.

Mum normally has a bag for him ready, which has our things that stay at his house, things that we have snuck over, and she has found decluttering, or clothes that we have worn over that belong at his house. If he has cycled Dad carries the bag and Hattie will walk with him and I ride his bike back. Mum hates it when I do that because it is a massive bike, and I don't have my helmet.

Dad only lives two streets away from Mum, so it is really easy for us to go in between for an evening, as it only takes a few minutes to get there. We have friends who live halfway between us, just past the alleyway.

Uncle Monkey is my Godfather, and he lives in the corner house at the end of the cul-de-sac and has his daughter Imelda come to stay sometimes. She is Hattie's best friend. Then on the other end of that row, at the crossroads, Cheryl has her house and she lives there with her two daughters, Hollie and Lilyana, who are my best friends.

We always pester Dad, asking if we can play with them when we stay with him. He normally texts in the day to see if the girls are there so we can make a plan. Uncle Monkey has a massive trampoline in his garden, so we play on that quite a bit as well as playing in the cul-de-sac outside Dad's house and in each other's rooms.

Dad almost always gives us chicken, mash and broccoli or beans on toast for dinner. Dad and Mum have competitions to see who does the best mash, we normally vote Dad as the winner. Hattie takes so long eating it, even though she likes it. This really annoys me because I'm not allowed to leave the table or get pudding until she has finished.

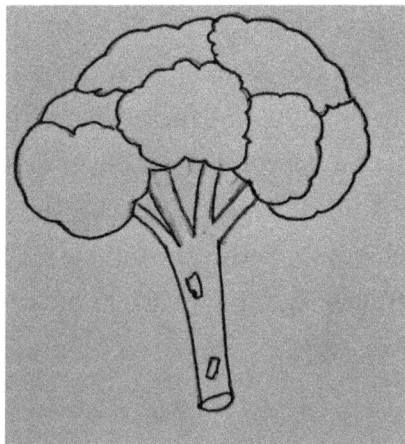

We have a shower and hair wash on Dad's evenings We always try to get that out of the way as soon as we get there, unless we have planned a sea swim. If we have, then we do that first and shower afterwards. Getting showered first gives us more time to play with our friends because we go back to Mum's at 8 o'clock...or slightly after as Dad is always late returning us.

We keep our bikes at Dad's, so sometimes we will scooter and cycle around outside his house. The road is really quiet, so it is pretty safe as long as we are careful of the junction and driveways. Because Mum is having an extension built, she gave Dad one of her old sheds for his garden. Uncle Monkey helped him move it. We put our things in there now. Before that, everything used to be stashed under his stairs or in the top corner of his lounge.

Mum still gets irritated by the fact he stores his motorbike and surf boards in the lounge. She doesn't understand how after living there for so long he hasn't built a garage or a massive shed on his second parking space to store it all. I think that's why she gave him her old one, just so some of the stuff could be stored out of our way. He'll have to move it when he turns it into my new bedroom anyway.

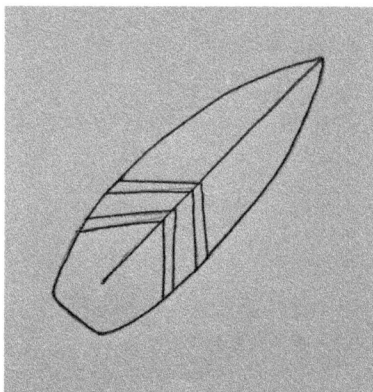

Dad's house is always trashed, he says it is us and that we make all the mess, but it isn't just that. Mum is always tidy and makes us sort our toys and bedroom out, so it is nice when we are at Dad's because we just throw all our clothes on the floor and leave all our stuff out and he doesn't care.

I think he does a big tidy about once a week, but it soon gets messed up again. He says part of the problem is

Mum declutters her house and gives it to him in case he needs it, and his house is smaller so has nowhere to put anything else. He gets so annoyed when she does that. He doesn't like sorting through stuff, so the bags get left on the stairs for ages.

Grandma and Aunty Sarah are coming from up country to visit us this weekend. Mum thinks Dad will do a massive tidy before they come and even get his motorbike out of the lounge too. I don't think he will. I'm looking forward to seeing them and am wondering if they will bring us any clothes or presents.

Weeknights always seem quite rushed at Dad's and if we are busy playing with our friends we never want to stop and go back to Mum's. Sometimes Cheryl leaves Hollie and Lilyana with us playing when she goes food shopping or to do the horses and if she isn't back before we head over then we all go to Mum's until they are collected from there.

Dad had a terrible story for us last night. I have been telling him for ages there was a weird smell in the kitchen. I was in there two nights ago making Lilyana a drink of squash and I was so embarrassed because it stunk so badly. Dad had tried cleaning out all the cupboards and surfaces, but he couldn't find anything.

Dad messaged us to say he found the source last night. Apparently, he got in from work and the stink was so overwhelming he had to open all the windows and doors to try to get it out of the house. He traced the smell to behind the fridge.

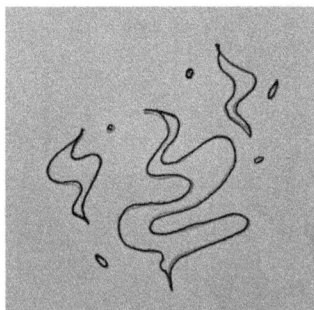

When Dad pulled it out, he found a collection tray next to the fridge motor. A mouse had set up home there. He thinks it must have been feeding on the cat's food and nestling in next to the heat. He said the tray was filled with a thousand mouse droppings and stinky rotting wee. When he was cleaning it, he was sick in the garden, it was so gross.

He found the mouse too. It was sat under his kitchen units, so he pulled out the skirting board and put the cat in there to catch it. Apparently, Gertie just went right up to it, sniffed it, and walked off again! Mum thinks the mouse has been there so long that it and the cat have made friends!

Dad said the mouse has now escaped in the house somewhere. He has asked to borrow one of Mum's rat catchers. Mum uses them around the rabbit hutch in the garden at home in case rats try to get to the food. When we catch one, we take it down to the field and let it out so it can't find its way back. I hope we can catch the mouse this weekend, it will be so cute.

Chapter 5

Weekend Mum

We always get a really good lie-in when we sleep at Mum's for the weekend. It is so quiet in our house because it is in the end of a cul-de-sac and one side of our house backs onto a stream and woodland. Mum doesn't get up early either, so she doesn't wake us moving about. Hattie is normally the first to wake up.

The no screens rule goes out of the window on the weekend, so we put our tablets on when we wake up and watch them in bed or on the sofa in our pj's for a bit until breakfast. Sometimes we put the TV on whilst we eat, but mostly we keep our tablets on the table with our headphones connected, watching kid's YouTube.

It is nice not having to rush about like we do for school days. Hattie doesn't have her swimming lesson until 10am on a Saturday, so it gives us loads of time to chill out before we go to that. The Sports Centre is only about ten minutes away in the car, but Mum always leaves really early so we get there before the lesson starts. She doesn't like to be late for stuff.

Hattie is in the big pool now and does full lengths in her lessons. I don't go anymore because I reached the top group, so I swapped to do surf lifesaving instead. I usually do my homework when Hattie is in the pool, it gets it out of the way then so that we can just have fun for the rest of the time off school.

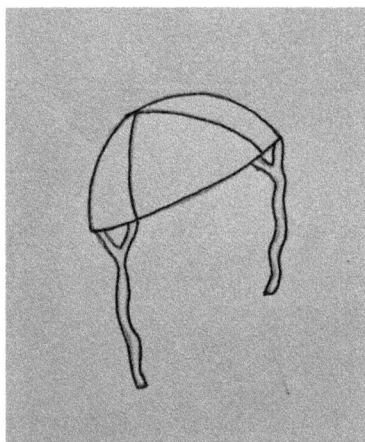

Mum always plans stuff for the weekends, so we normally have a day trip adventure to go on. Mum normally has to plan this around a birthday though, because one of us quite often has a party to go to. The parties are normally on a Saturday afternoon.

When we have a full day to play with, because there isn't a party, Mum will organise things like a beach day, woodland walk, theme park, open top bus trip, play dates with friends or a show somewhere. There is always something fun for us to do.

Sometimes on a Saturday evening we walk over to the village pub and meet friends. It's really good in the Summer because they have live music on the stage in the beer garden and there is a big play area out there too and a big field that we can run about in next to the car park. Mum usually arranges for us to meet friends there; we have some food and Mum has some beer with the grown-ups and chats with them whilst we all play.

We don't stay there too late because Mum likes us to be in bed by 9 o'clock. I get up early for surf lifesaving on a Sunday morning. We have to be on the beach at 9:15am to register and help bring down the boards from the clubhouse. We usually have the session for about an hour, sometimes a little longer, we have training in the water and also beach stuff too, like sprints, relays and my favourite game called flags.

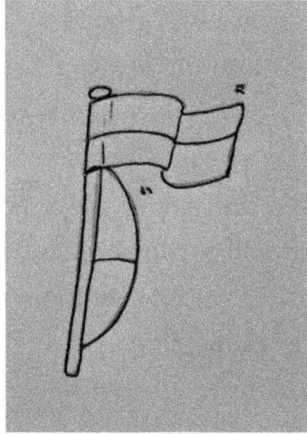

Mum and Hattie play on the beach whilst I am training. They aren't allowed in the water. This is in case there is an emergency and I need help; the instructors need to be able to find Mum quickly. We have to wear special caps in the sessions so we can be spotted easily, our team colours are yellow, red, and blue.

Last weekend we spent the entire two days on Holywell Beach. I took part in my first ever surf lifesaving competition. There was a lot of waiting around between my races, but it was good fun playing with my team and also friends from school who were in other teams racing against us.

Mum was super proud of me for doing the sea swimming race. The water was so rough that instead of swimming out and across and back in again like a 'n' shape, they had to change it to a 'm' shape to give us a chance to swim in with the waves and get our breath back. I completed it, but when I got out, I couldn't even speak, I just made a weird sound for ages. Mum was laughing, I was so shaken up - like I had been swimming in a washing machine, I was like jelly.

We normally call in and visit Nanny and Grandpa on a Sunday or call them to meet up with us for a walk somewhere and an ice cream or sometimes we go crabbing at the river near to their house. Grandpa doesn't come with us that often because he gets a bad back standing around. He comes when we go sea swimming though and he gets in the water with us.

If our cousins and uncles are visiting from Weston-s-Mare, then we always meet up with them for lunch out somewhere and a walk. Then we all hang out at Nanny and Grandpa's house. Our cousins who visit us from Weston are all grown-ups now, but they still come down and play with us when they visit.

Mum has three older brothers and the youngest of them lives in Australia. I like it best when he visits because my cousins come too, and they are nearer to my age. We have a really fun time playing together. I am always so sad when they go back though and get really upset about them leaving and saying goodbye.

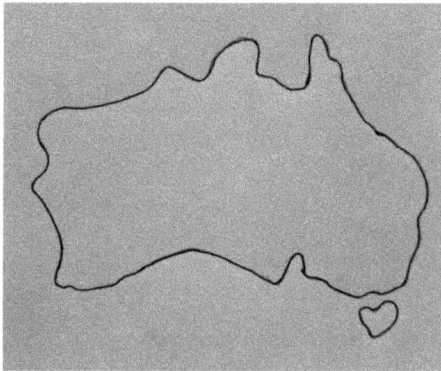

If we don't have family visiting, then we will normally have a chilled time on a Sunday evening with Mum. We have a roast dinner and then watch a movie, and play some games like Harry Potter, Pictionary Air, or Uno, or Nintendo Switch. Then we have a bath and hair washes and get an early night with a story, so we are rested for school the next day. We are reading David Walliams' book 'The Ice Monster' at the moment. Mum reads to us at night and does all the voices and sometimes we dip in and read a paragraph each too.

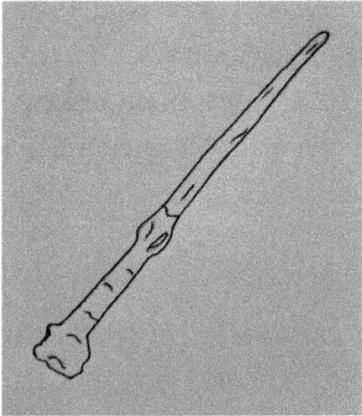

Chapter 6

Weekend Dad

Dad wakes up really early every single day, including the weekends. We all sleep upstairs at the moment; Dad has a mattress in the walk-in wardrobe that he sleeps in when we are there. Hattie and I sleep next to each other in the main bedroom in single beds. Dad sleeps in mine when we are with Mum.

He wakes up and tries to creep out and downstairs, but he usually disturbs us. Hattie gets up with him and I try to go back to sleep. Sometimes I can, but sometimes I end up getting up too. Dad does TV yoga in the mornings, so we sometimes join in. Otherwise, we sit on the sofa under a blanket and watch our iPads.

Dad always makes us pancakes for breakfast with sugar and honey on them. He makes them from scratch. Gertie is always meaowing at his feet to be fed and gets on his nerves because he nearly trips over her. We eat breakfast on the sofa, Mum never, ever, lets us do that in case we spill our food on it.

Even though we have been up for hours at Dad's we are still only just on time for Hattie's swimming lessons, sometimes we are late and get there when everyone is already in the pool. Mum gives Dad a 'club tub' for the weekend, that literally has everything in there that he needs for the lessons and surf lifesaving, but he still isn't organised to find all the bits ready to get there on time.

He gets so stressed trying to get us ready and out of the door. He says sorting clothes is the worst thing to have to do. I've tried helping and gone through all the drawers before for him, but they just get all messed up again because he doesn't know which is mine and which is Hattie's or even if what we have fits us anymore. One time he asked Mum to go over and sort the chest of drawers out for him, she said, 'Absolutely no way!' She thought he was ridiculous for not being able to do it himself, that's why I tried to help.

When Dad has us for the weekend, we normally go to the park and take our bikes in his car so we can use the pump track, or have fun swimming. There is a place called Pine Lodge which has an outdoor pool, and we like to go there on a sunny day too.

Uncle Monkey has Imelda on the same weekends that we are with Dad so we always hang out together. One time we went out on his boat along the river, and we had dolphins swimming next to us, it was so nice.

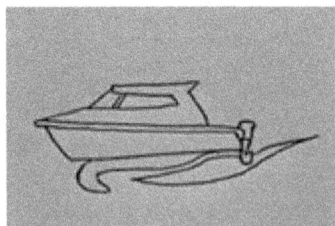

We have Camel Creek passes, so Dad sometimes takes us there too. It is a theme park that is only about twenty minutes away. We love the rides, and they have a 5D cinema, where you sit in a boat thing, and it moves you about when you are watching a movie with your 3D glasses on.

We can go there even if it is raining because they have pet areas, stables for horses, reptile houses and for bugs too which are all indoors. They also have a really big soft play and although I am getting a bit bored of the climbing bits now, they have death slides at Camel Creek and I will never be bored with those, they are so fast. It took me ages to be brave enough to do the biggest demon drop, but I find it easy now.

On a Saturday night, we usually go to Uncle Monkey's house. He has a fire pit, and we toast marshmallows. He also has a big trampoline that we play on. Hattie and Imelda normally just play up in her bedroom, so if Hollie and Lilyana don't come over, sometimes I get a bit bored.

The weekends used to be aligned so Hollie and Lilyana were with their Mum Cheryl on Dad's weekend, but it recently got switched and hasn't been changed back yet. It makes it hard for me because Dad wants to hang out with Monkey all the time and Imelda plays with Hattie, and I get left out.

We stay up really late when we are with Dad, he doesn't have the same rules as Mum, and sometimes we don't leave Uncle Monkeys until just before 10 at night. Mum says that's why she makes us go to bed early on a Sunday when we get back, to make up for the late night during term time so we aren't too tired for school. She isn't bothered during school holidays.

Sometimes Uncle Monkey shows me how to make things. He is doing up his house and changing it all about.

He does all the work himself, so he shows me and lets me help with some bits. I like doing that because it gives me something to do when we are hanging out over there.

Dad takes me to surf lifesaving on Sunday morning. Sometimes Hattie goes over to Uncle Monkeys to play with Imelda or take their dog 'Woof' for a walk whilst we are at the beach. We haven't been late for that yet, but there is always the same stress of getting the bits together from the club tub, that I need for the session. The other day he forgot to sign me out and lost my cap all on the same session. Mum had to buy another one.

Dad takes us into the town quite a bit too. We have our 'HyperJar' bank cards that Mum puts ten pounds a month on for us as pocket money, from her and Dad. If we have any leftover birthday money, she puts that on there too and we can just buy what we like with it. We normally get art stuff from The Works, jewellery from Claire's and crystals from Razmataz.

Last weekend Grandma and Aunty Sarah came to visit us. They stayed in the Premier Inn around the corner from Dad's house. We spent all weekend with them. We went sea swimming and Aunty Sarah even came in, we saw the poppy fields and Dad took photos with his proper camera and we went into town and bought some clothes.

We went to the village pub with them on Saturday night for dinner and Uncle Monkey and Imelda came too. We played in the play area, and they had drinks. I think we were very late to bed that night, but Mum didn't mind because it was a special occasion with Dad's family visiting, it just meant earlier to bed for us on the Sunday to make up for it.

They haven't been down for ages because it is a really long drive. We have visited them a few times though. It is normally really sad when we leave, but we weren't sad this time because we knew we would be seeing them in a few weeks when we go up with Dad in the Summer holidays.

Chapter 7

Nanny and Grandpa's

During term time when Mum is working Monday until Thursday, we go to Nanny and Grandpa's house for breakfast. Mum used to drop us off still in our pyjamas and take our school stuff with us, but Nanny would get too stressed out with us not getting dressed on time, so now we get our uniform on before we get dropped off.

Nanny gives us a sensible breakfast before school. We normally have cereal or toast. During school holidays, or on weekends and after school she makes up for it though with ice creams, pancakes, cakes, biscuits, and all sorts of treats.

Nanny and Grandpa live in a big bungalow near the boating lake. We have the end bedroom, which has twin beds. There is a really big, fitted wardrobe in there and it has all our toys in it. We have a really big doll's house and Sylvania family sets, puzzles, books, and art things.

Grandpa has two really scary full-head masks that my uncles used to wear on skiing holidays to frighten people. They used to be kept in the toy wardrobe in our bedroom, but I was so frightened of them that I had to get them moved. I'm still terrified of seeing them now, even in the old photos. Nanny said they threw them out, but I think they have them hidden somewhere else in the house.

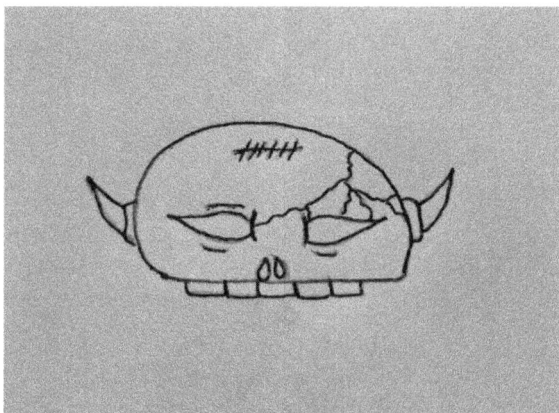

If Mum is running late to pick us up after she finishes work, Nanny will collect us from school. Grandpa usually drives her and drops us off because parking is a real nightmare at pick up time. If Mum has a conference or work meeting, we stay overnight so Nanny and Grandpa can do the school runs.

Sometimes Mum has made plans on her weekend with us. She might go out for dinner with friends, or to the silent disco, or watch a band. If she is drinking, then we stay at Nanny and Grandpa's house. If Mum has gone into town, sometimes she stays there with us too, because it is easier for her to walk there than get a taxi home.

We get to stay up late when we stay there. We sometimes watch a film on Nanny's laptop or watch our iPads in bed. We don't stay in the lounge very late because they watch their boring programs on the TV.

Sometimes Grandpa is in a really silly mood and gets on the floor and plays games with us. We like to play junior scrabble there too. Grandpa especially likes to try challenges. He is eighty four years old, but he likes to see if he can still do things. This one time we had to all try and do a gymnastics floor roll for our homework and film it and he got on the floor and was trying to do it, and another time he just started running in a car park, just to see if he could still sprint!

Sometimes he takes his false teeth out and we take pictures on our iPads of him doing funny gurning faces. Nanny only has a little plate with one missing tooth on it, but when she forgets to put it in, she is horrified and won't smile or talk to people in case they notice. She had to have her front tooth filed down once because it was growing too long. Before she had it fixed, we would call her Nanny McPhee, she hated that!

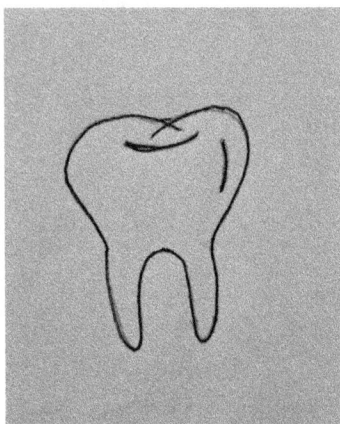

When we stay for a longer time with them, we go to National Trust houses on their memberships. We like doing trips out with them and always get an ice cream wherever we go. We normally go to the boating lake with the bird seed and feed the ducks. There is a café down there, so we get ice creams there too. This one time I don't think Nanny realised, but we had three ice creams in one day because we had two out and one from her freezer stash.

Grandpa is still really active and is always busy doing jobs. He still comes out to our house and does our gardening. He even climbs up the really tall ladder at his house to paint the top of their bungalow every couple of years and cleans the guttering. Nanny gets so stressed when he does that, she is always telling him off for doing too much and that he will kill himself one day by doing such dangerous things at his age.

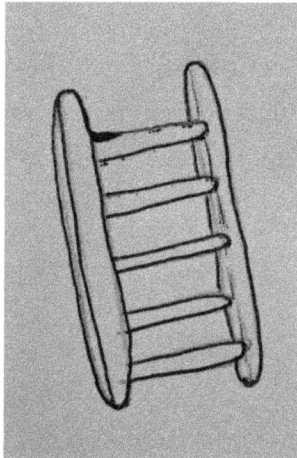

Nanny does all the cooking, she always makes us our favourite food when we go there, usually something with chips that she has done in her air fryer. Grandpa can cook bacon, but that's about it, I think. One time he had to ring Nanny when she was away to ask how to make scrambled eggs! He survives on ready meals if she isn't there to cook for him. They have been married forever, so I guess he has never had to learn.

Chapter 8

Holidays

Both Mum and Dad get holiday days that they can take off from work. They share it out so they can look after us during the school holidays. When they have run out of days we stay with Nanny and Grandpa instead. We haven't been to another country since before Mum and Dad split up, but we do go away to nearby places.

My favourite place to go is Butlins at Minehead. We have been two years in a row now, but Mum said she can't face it again next year, so we are going to go to London instead. We are going to visit Harry Potter

World, the Science Museum, go on an open-top bus tour and maybe see a show. I can't wait for that.

We went glamping with Mum to Tavistock the other week and then had a trip to Weston-s-Mare to see friends and family too. These next two weeks Dad has got us, so we are travelling up to Rugby to see our family there. That is such a massive drive, but we put the screens up with the DVD player connected so at least we can watch movies.

Mum is more organised than Dad when it comes to travelling, so when we are with her, we go away to places, but when we are with Dad we generally stay around Newquay and do stuff here instead. He didn't really even want to go to Rugby because he said there is nothing to do there, but Mum suggested day trips to places like Stratford and how important it was for us to see his family, and then he got excited.

I really want to go to Australia again to stay with my cousins. We went before Mum and Dad split up. Mum said if she has any spare money after the extension then maybe we could put it towards a trip out there the following Easter, I really hope that happens. We wouldn't go next year because they are hoping to visit us in June and July anyway and Mum likes to spread out the visits.

We don't go to Weston that much, but when we do I love it. We ride on the donkeys, play on the pier, on the two pence machines and see our friends. Mum has three best mates that she always meets up with and they all have girls too and we all play together whilst they chat grown-up stuff.

I have two uncles there and grown-up cousins and we always hang out with them and have a nice time. We see them a lot more than Dad's family though. They come down to visit us in Newquay a lot because it is so much closer, only about a two-hour drive I think, instead of six to Rugby.

This time we went to Wookey Hole caves on a day trip. It was so good. They have a 4D cinema experience there and you get blasted with air from the chair and things grab your legs from underneath and poke at your back and bottom. Everyone was screaming with surprise, it was so much fun.

It absolutely poured it down with rain when we were leaving and we tried to play the mini golf because it was part of the ticket price, but it was flooded and we got stuck trying to get around. Mum had to pick us up to carry us over the deep puddles. We only got to play on two of the holes.

I really liked the old penny slot machines there too. They were saved from an old pier, and you have to change your money into old money to use them. There are fortune teller ones there and I did three of them. One of them reads your palm and you can feel the machine rippling under your skin as it searches and then a card pops out of the bottom with your fortune.

I am looking forward to going to Rugby. Grandma lives on a sheep farm, and we love playing with all the kittens. They aren't pets, they are there to keep the rats away, so we can't ever catch them, but it is fun trying. Grandma's husband has lots of old tractors in a barn too and we always sit on them and choose our favourites.

It is sad that Grandad isn't alive anymore as we used to always see him and Nana Maureen when we went up. I bet we will drive past his old house though for memory's sake, I just hope I don't get too sad when we do. Daddy has two sisters who live up there, so we will see them and also our cousins.

Our cousins in Rugby are all grown up, but they have children similar ages to us, so we love playing with them and having pictures taken for the memory albums. Mum likes to keep these photos at her house so when we are older, we can look back on our family visits.

We stay in Newquay for Christmas. Mum and Dad normally end up arguing during the holiday at some point. We used to all go to Nanny and Grandpa's house for Christmas dinner. We did that even after Mum and Dad split up, but Mum said she couldn't relax with him there, and so she changed it, we don't have it together anymore.

Now Mum has us Christmas Eve and Christmas Day and we go to Nanny and Grandpa's for cooked dinner and stay overnight there so Mummy can have a drink and chill out. Then Boxing Day morning, we go to Dad's for a couple of days and have a second Christmas day there.

Last year Dad had Uncle Monkey and Imelda there too, so we had a big Christmas lunch and opened all our gifts from Dad's family then. We keep all of those presents at Dad's house and the ones we opened at Mum's, from her family, we keep there.

Mum said we will do it like this whilst Nanny and Grandpa are still alive, so we all get to spend Christmas lunch together as she has every year since she was born. After they die, I think we will probably take it in turns each year like other split families do. Dad seems happy with the arrangement as it is because he gets to go out to the pub drinking with his friends on Christmas Eve and then has Christmas lunch with Uncle Monkey and more beer.

The good thing about having two houses is that Father Christmas comes to both, so we get two stockings. I know he doesn't exist, but we keep the secret alive for Hattie as she is still a believer. Mum said the minute we both know he isn't real he won't come anymore, so that is a good bribe to make sure I don't tell Hattie.

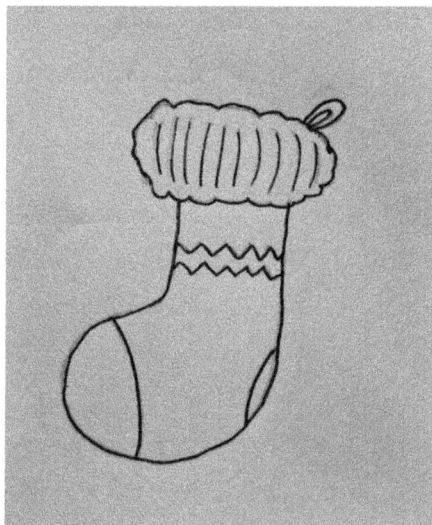

One Christmas Mum and Dad had a massive argument. They normally try to hide it from us and don't like to talk about serious stuff in front of us. Mum was trying to get hold of us on Boxing Day night and she was really worried Dad had drunk too much and left the Christmas tree lights on, she just got it in her head and started panicking.

Mum came over to check and it was really late, and we were all still having a party with our friends. Mum marched upstairs to check on us and Dad followed her, and she started shouting at him for not answering his phone and how worried she had been. Dad went crazy and started yelling and swearing in her face. It was so bad. Uncle Monkey took him downstairs, and I was crying.

Mum told us it was ok and not to listen to what words were being said by the grown-ups and not to let it ruin the fun and that she was just worried, and Daddy was angry that she marched in and got cross, and it was grown up stuff and nothing for us to worry about.

Once we were settled and happy to keep playing with our friends she left. I heard her ask Uncle Monkey to make sure the tree lights were turned off before he left them and then she burst into tears and walked home.

I never want to see that happen again. My friends were there at the time and when I spoke to them about it, they said their Mum and Dad had had way worse rows than that and not to worry about it. That made me feel better.

Mum spoke to me about it a couple of days later and explained why she was worried and that she was sorry it happened in front of us and she wished she had done it differently, but also wanted us to know that this is why they are no longer married, because she didn't want us growing up in a house where arguments like that would and could happen a lot.

Apparently, a lot of families have arguments around Christmas time. Something to do with lots of different people coming together, but they expect it to be full of fun and they drink too much and spend too much money on presents and food just for one day. It puts the pressure on, and people just explode at each other.

Chapter 9

Turning 11 years old

When I turn eleven I will...

- Have a mobile phone
- Be in my last year of primary school
- Know if I got my secondary school choice
- Be one year older
- Be taller
- Have boobs
- Have a bra
- Have been to Harry Potter World
- Be seeing my Australian cousins very soon
- Be a higher belt at karate
- Be really good at surf life-saving
- Have lots more subscribers on my YouTube channel

- Have my own bedroom at Mum's house
- Be allowed to cross the busy road to the shop on my own

When I turn eleven I will not...

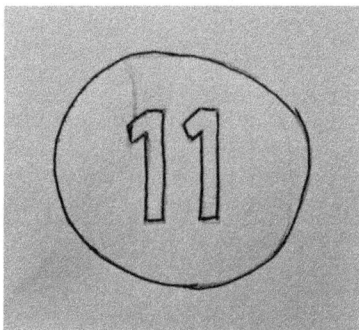

- Have my second piercing
- Be able to drive
- Have short hair
- Like peppers
- Have a dog

The End.

About The Author

Vicki Baxter lives by the Cornish coast with her two daughters.

Following her graduation with a Leisure Management and Sports degree, Vicki has experienced a varied career as a tennis coach, prison custody officer and sales representative in the confectionery market.

Vicki works four days a week and enjoys using her day off writing, cold water sea swimming and exercising. Vicki's previous publications include a rhyming picture and activity book called 'Our World and Me.' A children's fantasy story called 'The Hatteme Tales' (illustrated by Caz Banks and narrated by Kate Stebbing-Allen). A book about her previous work experience called 'Incarcerated – A Young Offender Institute Through the Eyes of an Officer,' and a selection of poetry in various books.

Vicki's inspiration to start writing came from composing poems for her friends at secondary school. This led to her Nan suggesting she enter one of them into a competition. 'The Perfect Wave' was a success and was published in a poetry collection. Writing has become a passion and something to give to her daughters as they grow up and have their own families.

www.blossomspringpublishing.com

www.ingramcontent.com/pod-product-compliance
Lightning Source LLC
Chambersburg PA
CBHW032025040426
42448CB00006B/729